HEY HIPPOPOTAMUS DO BABIES EAT CAKE TOO?

Hodder & Stoughton
SYDNEY AUCKLAND LONDON TORONTO

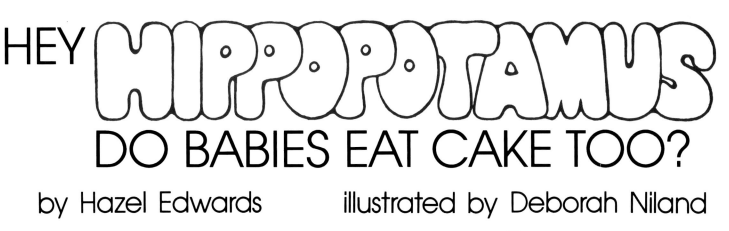

HEY HIPPOPOTAMUS

DO BABIES EAT CAKE TOO?

by Hazel Edwards   illustrated by Deborah Niland

For the Hogan family

First published in 1992 by
Hodder & Stoughton (Australia) Pty Limited
10-16 South Street, Rydalmere NSW 2116

Reprinted 1993 in hardback and paperback (twice)

Text copyright © Hazel Edwards, 1992
Illustrations copyright © Deborah Niland, 1992

National Library of Australia Cataloguing-in-Publication entry

Edwards, Hazel
    Hey hippopotamus, do babies eat cake too?
    ISBN 0 340 54969 6 hardback
    ISBN 0 340 58459 9 paperback
        1. Hippopotamus — Juvenile fiction.
        I. Niland, Deborah.   II. Title.
A823'.3

Printed in Hong Kong.

Mummy is having a baby.
She told me.
"When?" I ask.
"Soon," she says. "The baby will belong to all of us."

I've got a Daddy and a big brother, but we haven't
   had a baby before.
So I told my hippopotamus who lives on the roof
   and eats cake.
He knows everything about babies.

Then I ask Mummy, "Is our baby in your tummy now?"
She nods.
"Was I in your tummy too?"
"Yes."
'Why didn't I see the baby then?"
Mummy and Daddy laugh.
But my hippopotamus knows what I mean.

My brother and I play football.
"Will the baby be able to play football?" I ask.
"Not for a while," Daddy says.
My hippopotamus on the roof can play anything.

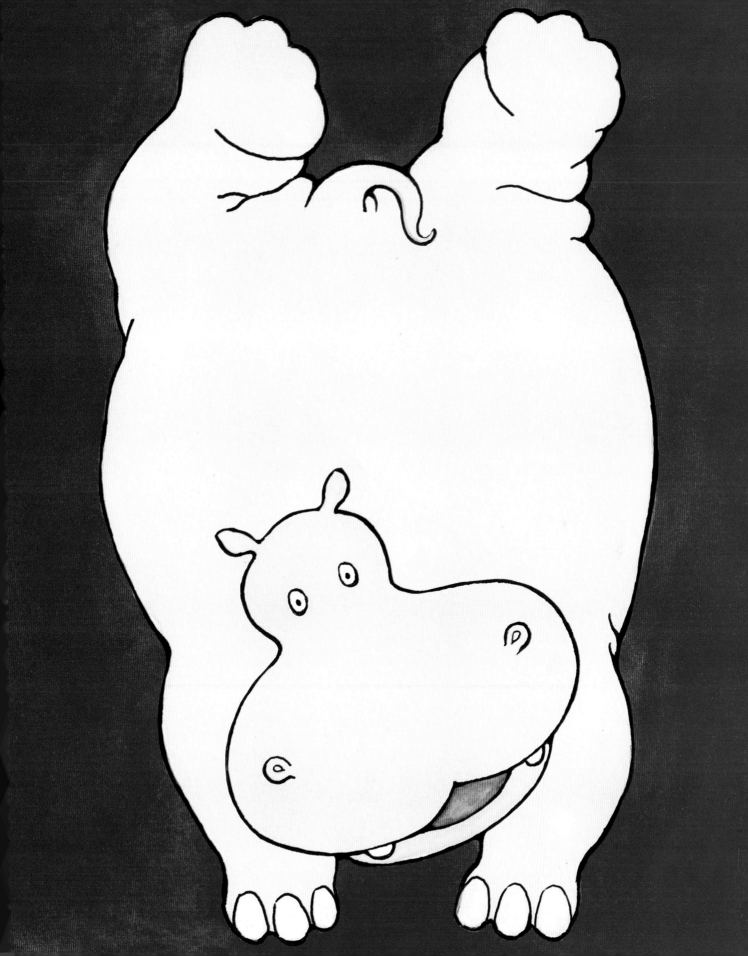

"What's the baby's name?"
Mummy smiles. "We haven't chosen a name yet."
That's all right.
My hippopotamus doesn't have a name.
But he's always there on the roof, eating cake.

Our baby has a room
and a cot
and a bath
and millions of nappies.
But the baby has no name.
We haven't chosen it yet.
My hippopotamus is thinking of a name.

Grandma is in the kitchen.
We make pizza.
She asks me, "Is the baby's name PIZZA?"
We laugh.
I say, "No!"

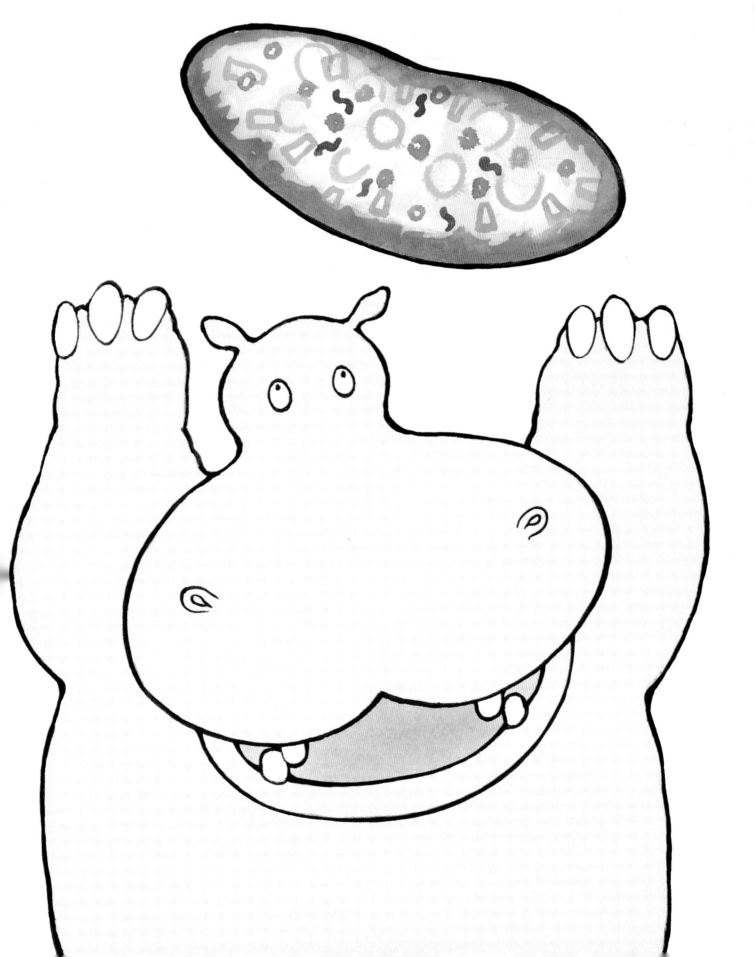

Aunty fixes my bike in the garage.
We make a mess.
She asks me, "Is the baby's name BIKE?"
We laugh.
I say, "No!"

Daddy paints the bedroom.
Paint falls on me.
I ask, "What colour will the baby be?"
"Wait and see," Daddy says.
My hippopotamus on the roof knows all *his* colours.

Daddy washes my hair.
It is wet and shiny.
I ask, "Will the baby have hair?"
"Wait and see," Daddy says.
My hippopotamus hasn't got any hair but he's got
   a lovely wig.

Grandpa reads me a story.
He takes off his glasses.
His eyes are brown.
I ask, "What colour will our baby's eyes be?"
"Wait and see."
My hippopotamus can see everything from up on
   the roof.

The man at the shop asks, "Do you want a brother
    or a sister?"
I don't know.
Sometimes I'd like to have a baby.
Other times I don't want one.
My hippopotamus wants the baby to look like me.

Uncle gives me a dolly in a cot.
"What's your dolly's name?" he asks.
I don't know yet.
Uncle smiles. "Is it a No-Name Dolly?"
I say, "Yes."
My hippopotamus knows *my* name because it's on
   my clothes.
And he *has* got a name really, but it's our secret.

Early this morning, Daddy woke me up.
"Our baby's here," he said.
I went to see the No-Name Baby.
It was red, squashy and beautiful.
Daddy told me the baby's name.
And it's just right.

Baby drinks only milk.
But my hippopotamus saved some cake for later.
He knows everything about babies.